BLACK PANTHER

A NATION UNDER OUR FEET: PART 6

ABDOBOOKS.COM

Reinforced library bound edition published in 2020 by Spotlight, a division of ABDO, PO Box 398166, Minneapolis, Minnesota 55439. Spotlight produces high-quality reinforced library bound editions for schools and libraries. Published by agreement with Marvel Characters, Inc.

Printed in the United States of America, North Mankato, Minnesota.
042019   092019

THIS BOOK CONTAINS
RECYCLED MATERIALS

© 2020 MARVEL

Library of Congress Control Number: 2018965952

Publisher's Cataloging-in-Publication Data

Names: Coates, Ta-Nehisi, author. | Stelfreeze, Brian; Martin, Laura; Sprouse, Chris; Story, Karl, illustrators.
Title: A nation under our feet / writer: Ta-Nehisi Coates; art: Brian Stelfreeze ; Laura Martin ; Chris Sprouse ; Karl Story.
Description: Minneapolis, Minnesota : Spotlight, 2020 | Series: Black Panther
Summary: With a dramatic upheaval in Wakanda on the horizon, T'Challa knows his kingdom needs to change to survive, but he struggles to find balance in his roles as king and the Black Panther.
Identifiers: ISBN 9781532143519 (pt. 1 ; lib. bdg.) | ISBN 9781532143526 (pt. 2 ; lib. bdg.) | ISBN 9781532143533 (pt. 3 ; lib. bdg.) | ISBN 9781532143540 (pt. 4 ; lib. bdg.) | ISBN 9781532143557 (pt. 5 ; lib. bdg.) | ISBN 9781532143564 (pt. 6 ; lib. bdg.)
Subjects: LCSH: Black Panther (Fictitious character)--Juvenile fiction. | Superheroes--Juvenile fiction. | Kings and rulers--Juvenile fiction. | Graphic novels--Juvenile fiction. | T'Challa, of Wakanda (Fictitious character)--Juvenile fiction.
Classification: DDC 741.5--dc23

ABDO
Spotlight

A Division of ABDO
abdobooks.com

BLACK PANTHER

AFTER A SUICIDE BOMBER SEVERELY INJURED HIS MOTHER, T'CHALLA DECLARED WAR ON TETU'S REBELS. WITH THE HELP OF **MANIFOLD** AND THE **HATUT ZERAZE**, HE ORCHESTRATED RAIDS ON THEIR HIDEOUTS, MANAGING TO CAPTURE SEVERAL TERRORISTS OUTFITTED WITH REPULSOR BOMB BIOTECHNOLOGY.

AT AKILI'S BEHEST, A COUNTERREVOLUTION COUNCIL WAS CONVENED AND PRESENTED T'CHALLA WITH THE CRUELEST MEASURES FOR DEALING WITH A COUP. **TETU** AND **EZEKIEL STANE** LEAKED THE PARTICULARS OF THIS MEETING TO THE WORLD.

MEANWHILE, SHURI'S SPIRIT TRAVELS THE PLANE OF WAKANDAN MEMORY KNOWN AS THE DJALIA. SHE IS LED BY A GRIOT INHABITING THE VISAGE OF RAMONDA.

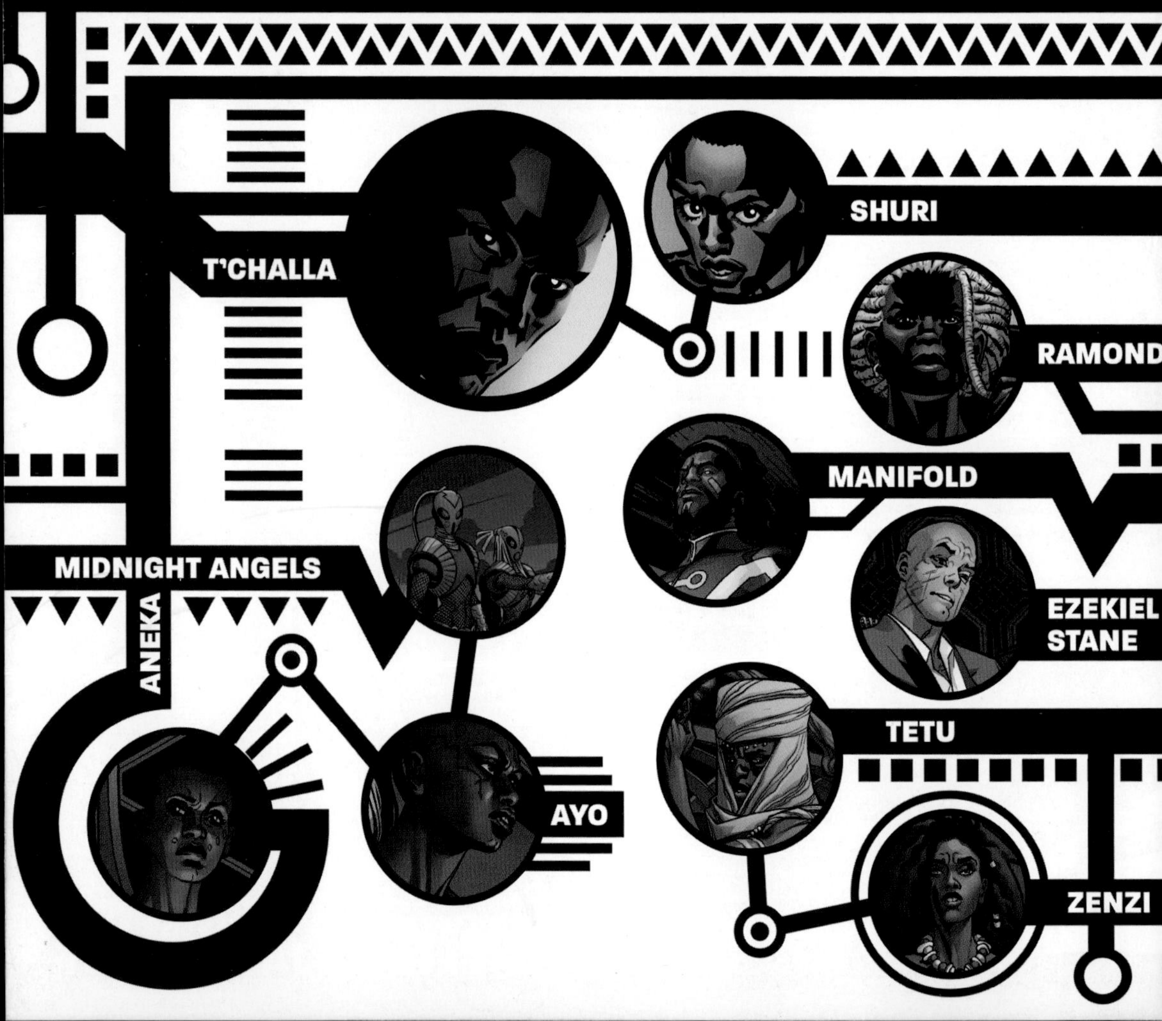

SHURI
T'CHALLA
RAMOND
MANIFOLD
MIDNIGHT ANGELS
ANEKA
EZEKIEL STANE
TETU
AYO
ZENZI

A NATION UNDER OUR FEET part 6

writer **TA-NEHISI COATES** penciler **CHRIS SPROUSE** inker **KARL STORY** color artist **LAURA MARTIN**

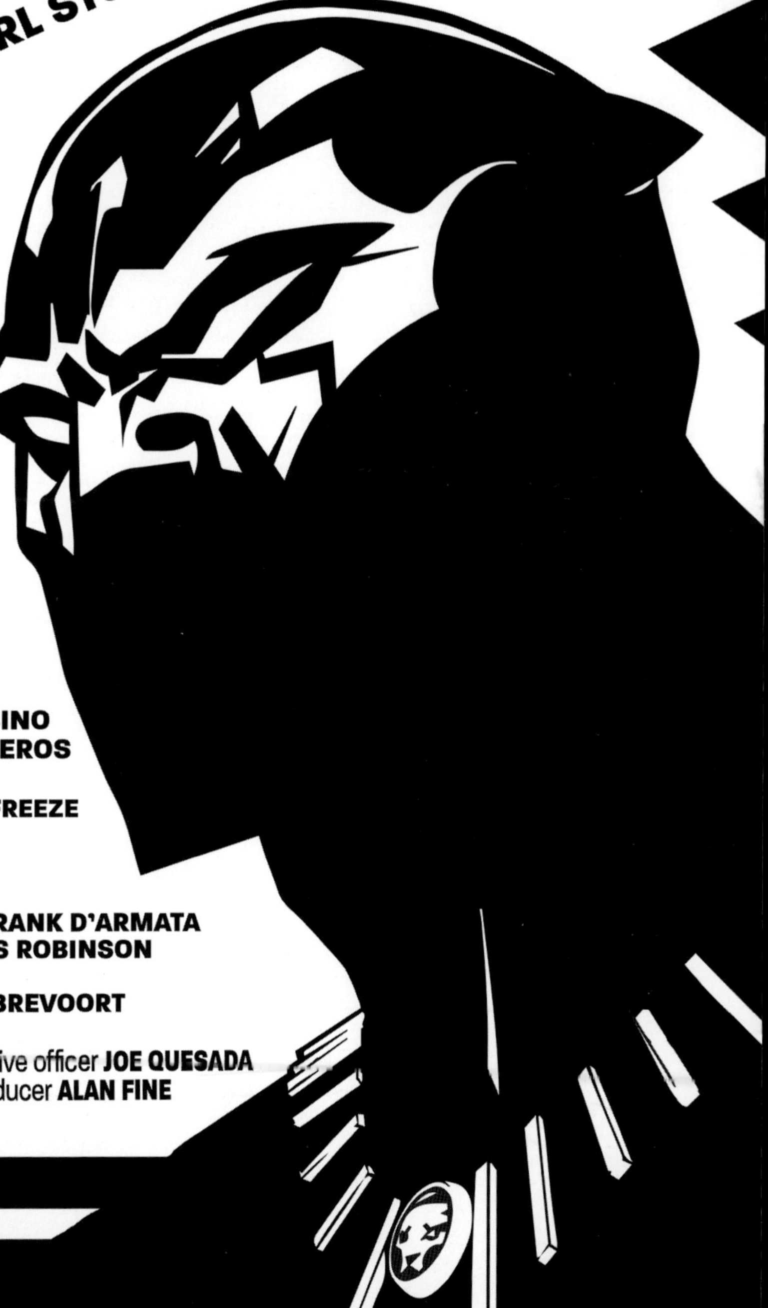

letterer **VC's JOE SABINO**
design **MANNY MEDEROS**
logo **RIAN HUGHES**
cover by **BRIAN STELFREEZE**
variant covers by
ESAD RIBIC
UDON
PASQUAL FERRY & **FRANK D'ARMATA**
assistant editor **CHRIS ROBINSON**
editor **WIL MOSS**
executive editor **TOM BREVOORT**

editor in chief **AXEL ALONSO** chief creative officer **JOE QUESADA**
publisher **DAN BUCKLEY** executive producer **ALAN FINE**

BLACK PANTHER created by **STAN LEE & JACK KIRBY**

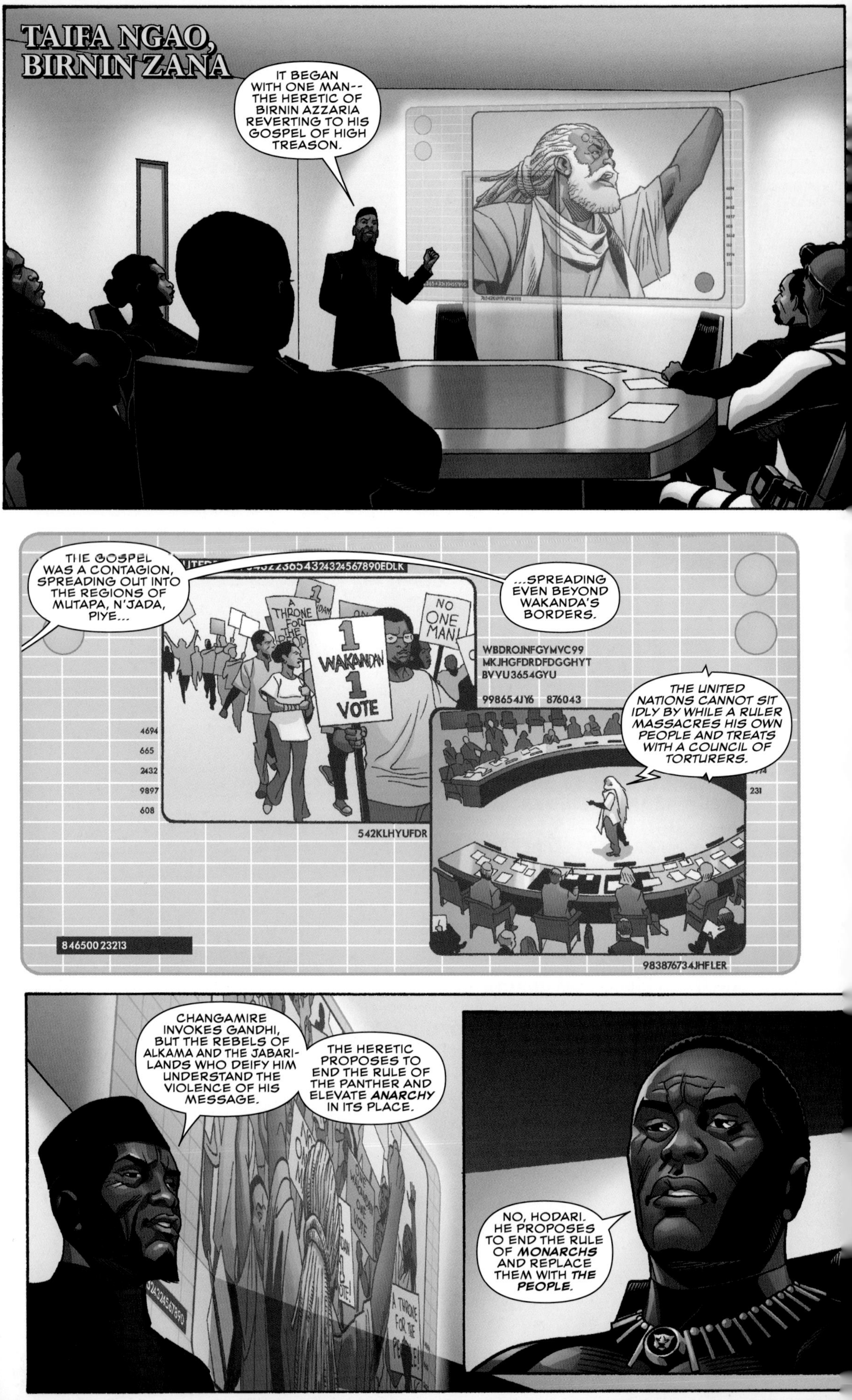
TAIFA NGAO, BIRNIN ZANA
IT BEGAN WITH ONE MAN-- THE HERETIC OF BIRNIN AZZARIA REVERTING TO HIS GOSPEL OF HIGH TREASON.
THE GOSPEL WAS A CONTAGION, SPREADING OUT INTO THE REGIONS OF MUTAPA, N'JADA, PIYE...
...SPREADING EVEN BEYOND WAKANDA'S BORDERS.
A THRONE FOR THE PEOPLE
NO ONE MAN!
1 WAKANDAN 1 VOTE
WBDROJNFGYMVC99
MKJHGFDRDFDGGHYT
BVVU3654GYU
998654JY6 876043
THE UNITED NATIONS CANNOT SIT IDLY BY WHILE A RULER MASSACRES HIS OWN PEOPLE AND TREATS WITH A COUNCIL OF TORTURERS.
542KLHYUFDR
8465002321 3
983876734JHFLER
CHANGAMIRE INVOKES GANDHI, BUT THE REBELS OF ALKAMA AND THE JABARI-LANDS WHO DEIFY HIM UNDERSTAND THE VIOLENCE OF HIS MESSAGE.
THE HERETIC PROPOSES TO END THE RULE OF THE PANTHER AND ELEVATE ANARCHY IN ITS PLACE.
NO, HODARI. HE PROPOSES TO END THE RULE OF MONARCHS AND REPLACE THEM WITH THE PEOPLE.

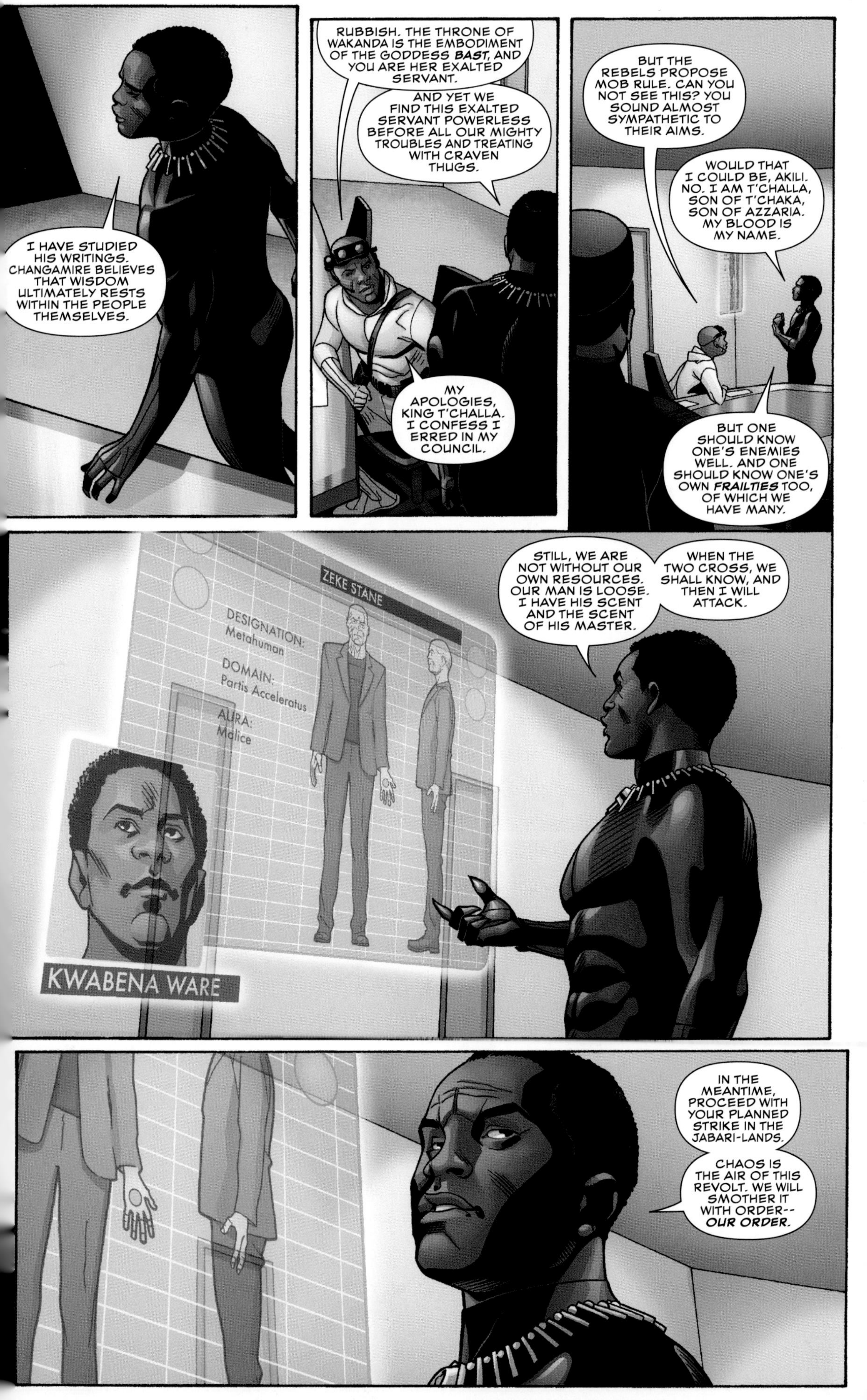
I HAVE STUDIED HIS WRITINGS. CHANGAMIRE BELIEVES THAT WISDOM ULTIMATELY RESTS WITHIN THE PEOPLE THEMSELVES.
RUBBISH. THE THRONE OF WAKANDA IS THE EMBODIMENT OF THE GODDESS BAST, AND YOU ARE HER EXALTED SERVANT.
AND YET WE FIND THIS EXALTED SERVANT POWERLESS BEFORE ALL OUR MIGHTY TROUBLES AND TREATING WITH CRAVEN THUGS.
MY APOLOGIES, KING T'CHALLA. I CONFESS I ERRED IN MY COUNCIL.
BUT THE REBELS PROPOSE MOB RULE. CAN YOU NOT SEE THIS? YOU SOUND ALMOST SYMPATHETIC TO THEIR AIMS.
WOULD THAT I COULD BE, AKILI. NO. I AM T'CHALLA, SON OF T'CHAKA, SON OF AZZARIA. MY BLOOD IS MY NAME.
BUT ONE SHOULD KNOW ONE'S ENEMIES WELL. AND ONE SHOULD KNOW ONE'S OWN FRAILTIES TOO, OF WHICH WE HAVE MANY.
ZEKE STANE
DESIGNATION: Metahuman
DOMAIN: Partis Acceleratus
AURA: Malice
KWABENA WARE
STILL, WE ARE NOT WITHOUT OUR OWN RESOURCES. OUR MAN IS LOOSE. I HAVE HIS SCENT AND THE SCENT OF HIS MASTER.
WHEN THE TWO CROSS, WE SHALL KNOW, AND THEN I WILL ATTACK.
IN THE MEANTIME, PROCEED WITH YOUR PLANNED STRIKE IN THE JABARI-LANDS.
CHAOS IS THE AIR OF THIS REVOLT. WE WILL SMOTHER IT WITH ORDER-- OUR ORDER.

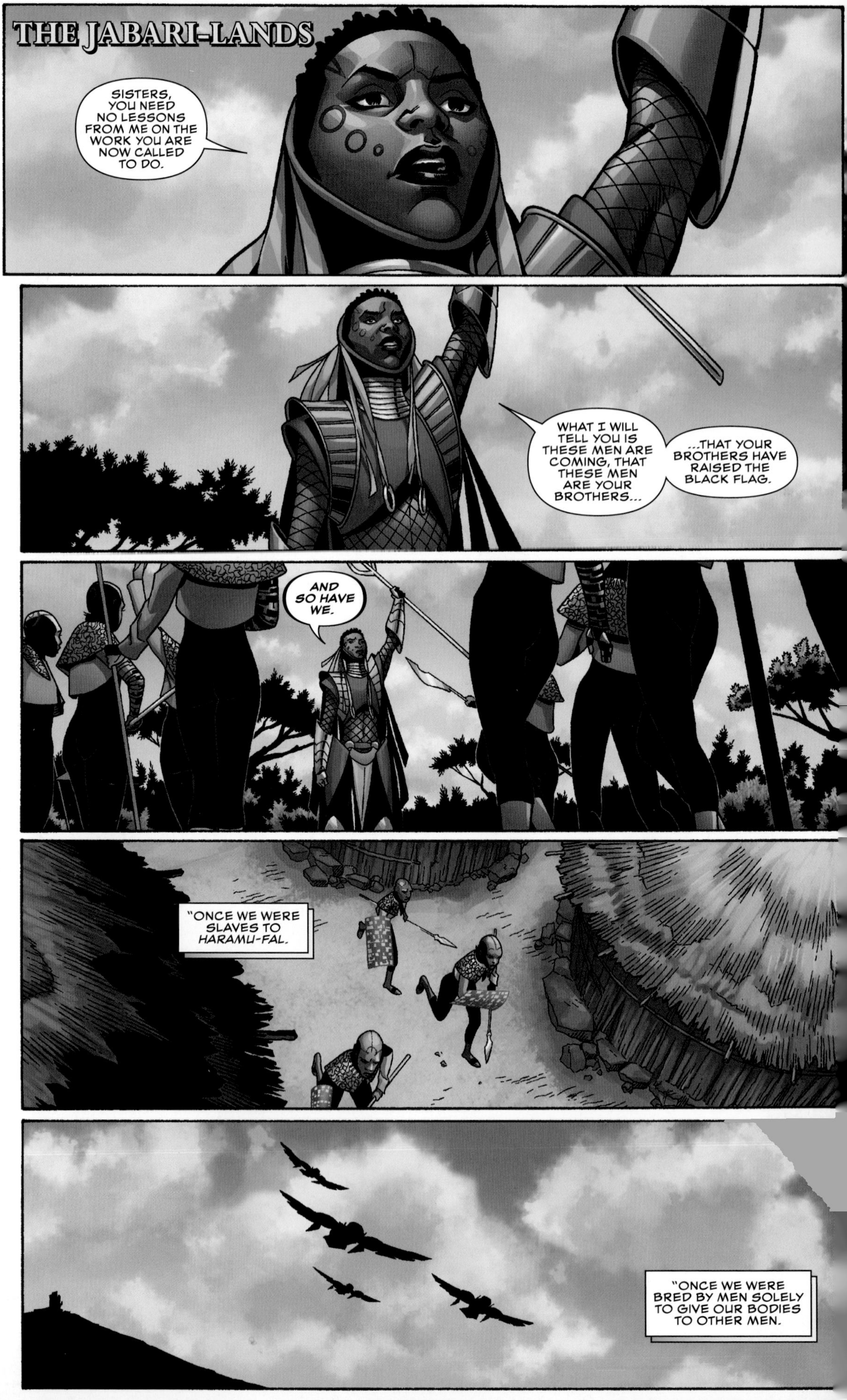
THE JABARI-LANDS
SISTERS, YOU NEED NO LESSONS FROM ME ON THE WORK YOU ARE NOW CALLED TO DO.
WHAT I WILL TELL YOU IS THESE MEN ARE COMING, THAT THESE MEN ARE YOUR BROTHERS...
...THAT YOUR BROTHERS HAVE RAISED THE BLACK FLAG.
AND SO HAVE WE.
"ONCE WE WERE SLAVES TO HARAMU-FAL.
"ONCE WE WERE BRED BY MEN SOLELY TO GIVE OUR BODIES TO OTHER MEN.

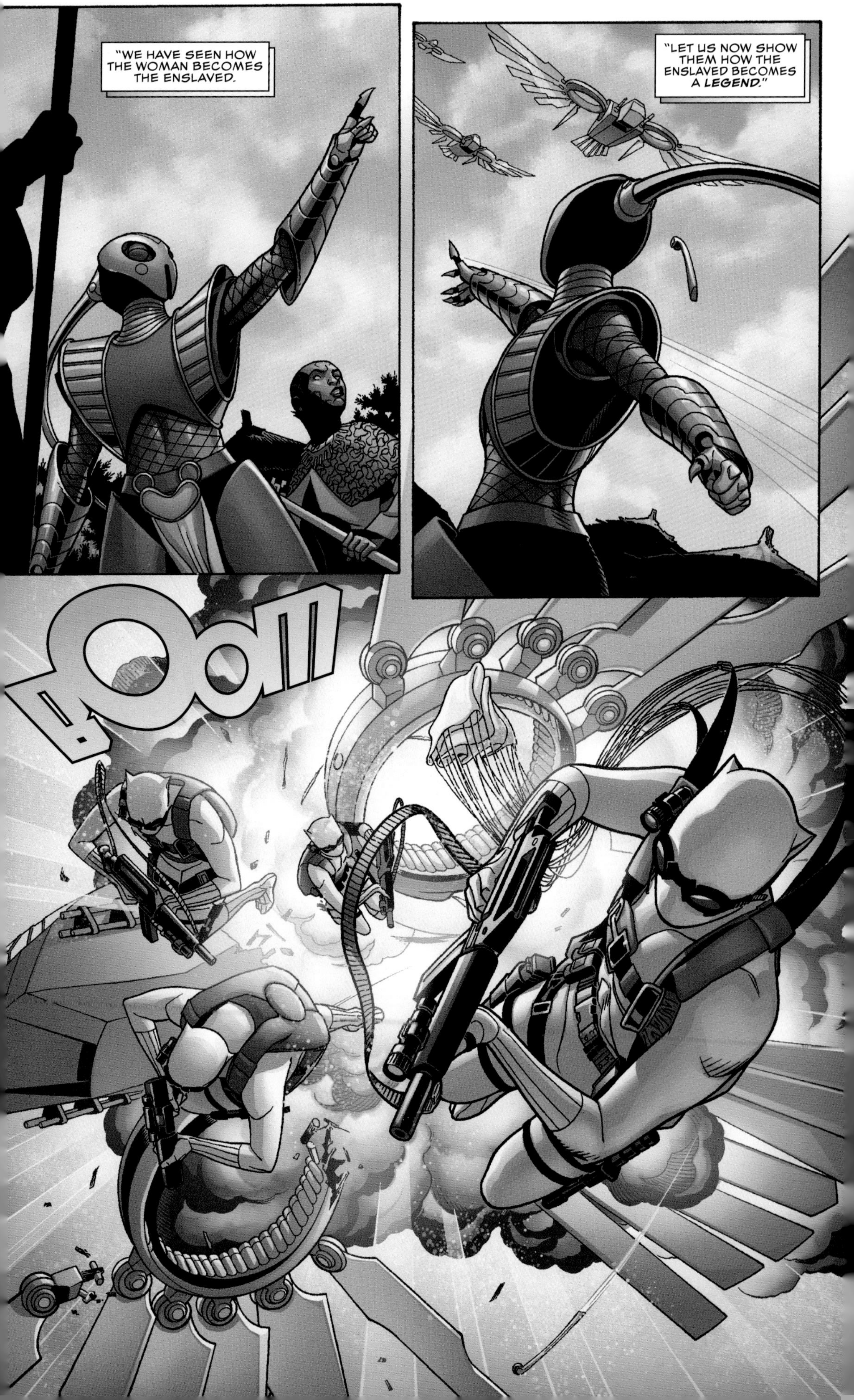
"WE HAVE SEEN HOW THE WOMAN BECOMES THE ENSLAVED.
"LET US NOW SHOW THEM HOW THE ENSLAVED BECOMES A *LEGEND*."
BOOM!

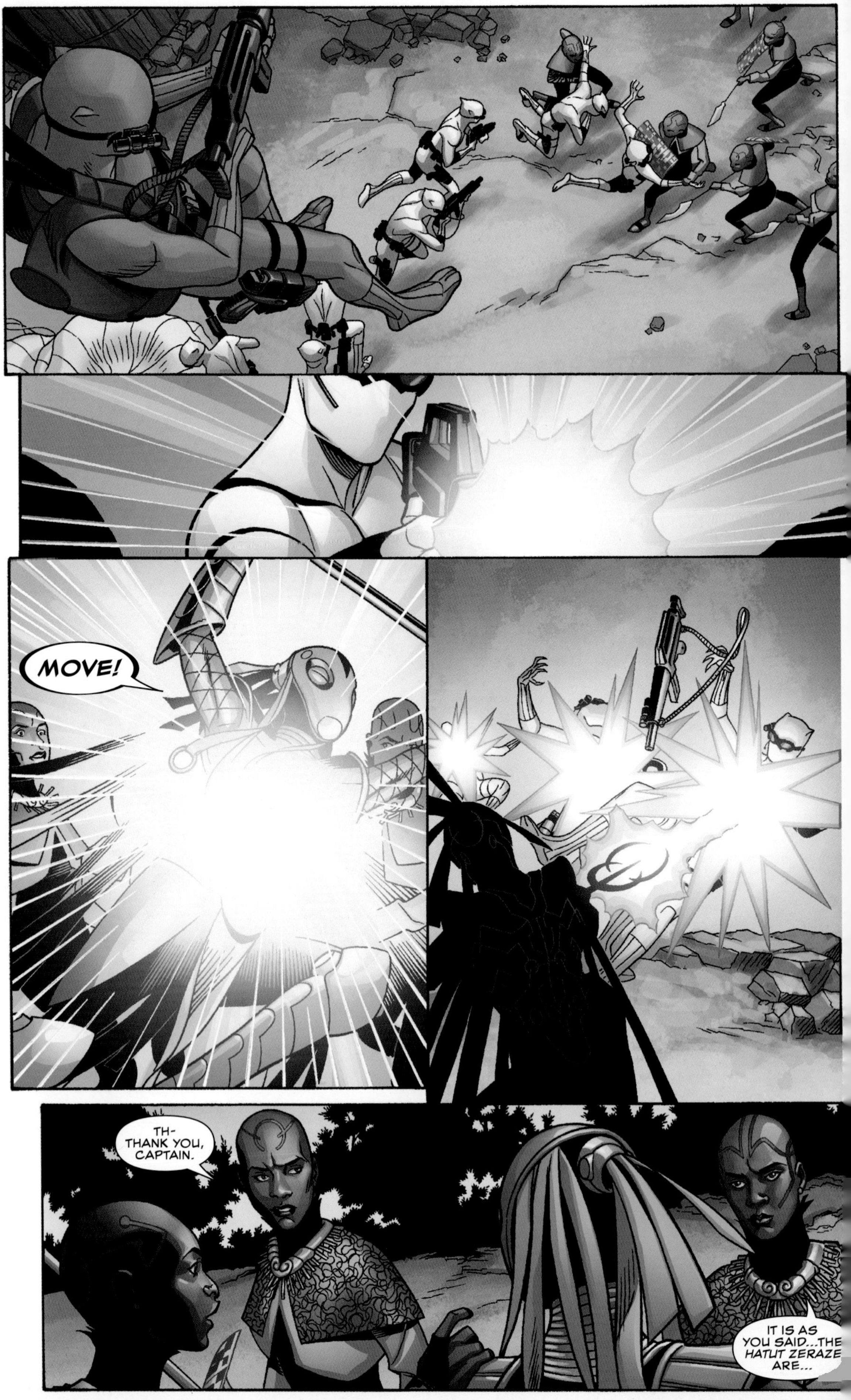
MOVE!
TH- THANK YOU, CAPTAIN.
IT IS AS YOU SAID... THE HATUT ZERAZE ARE...

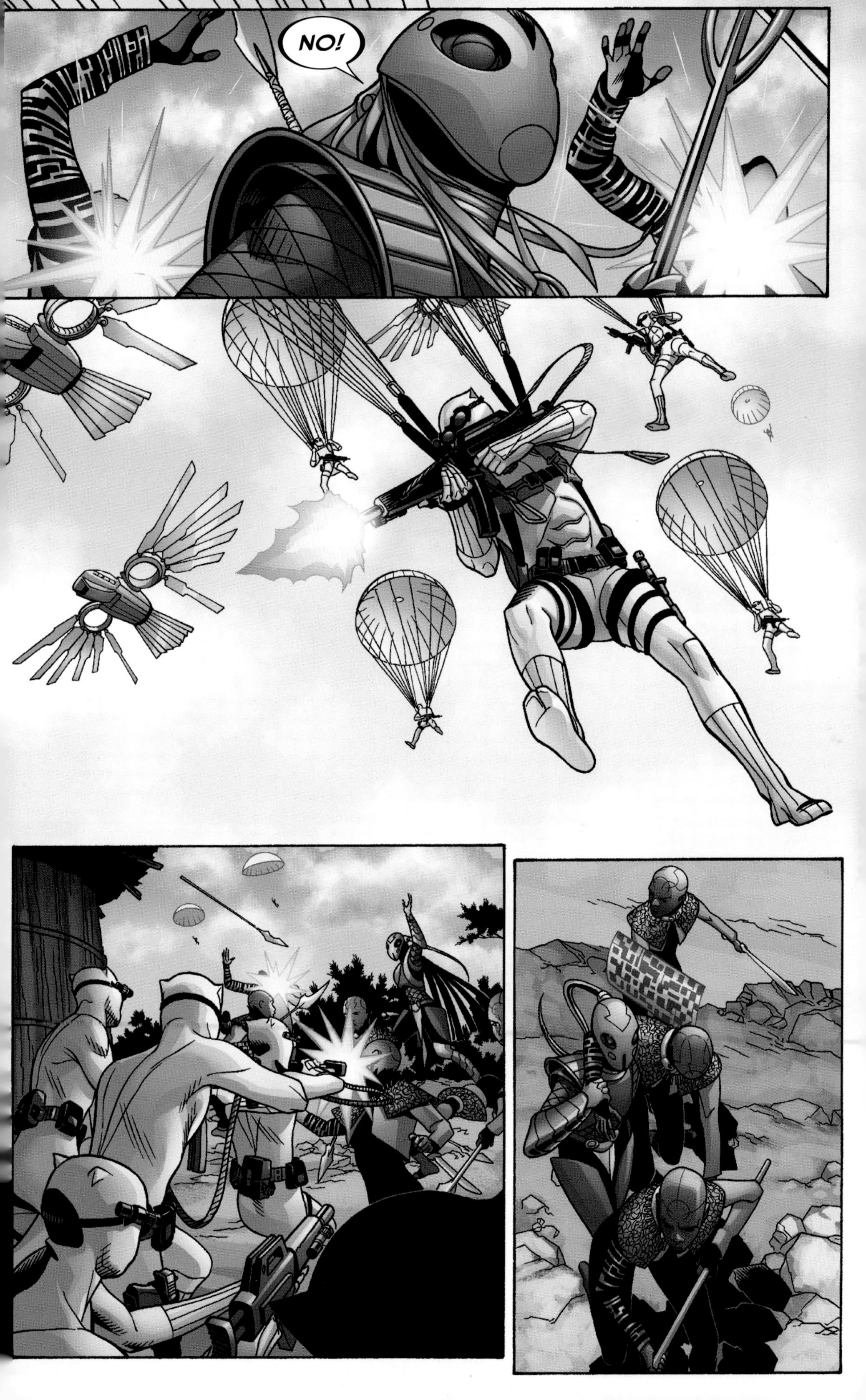
NO!

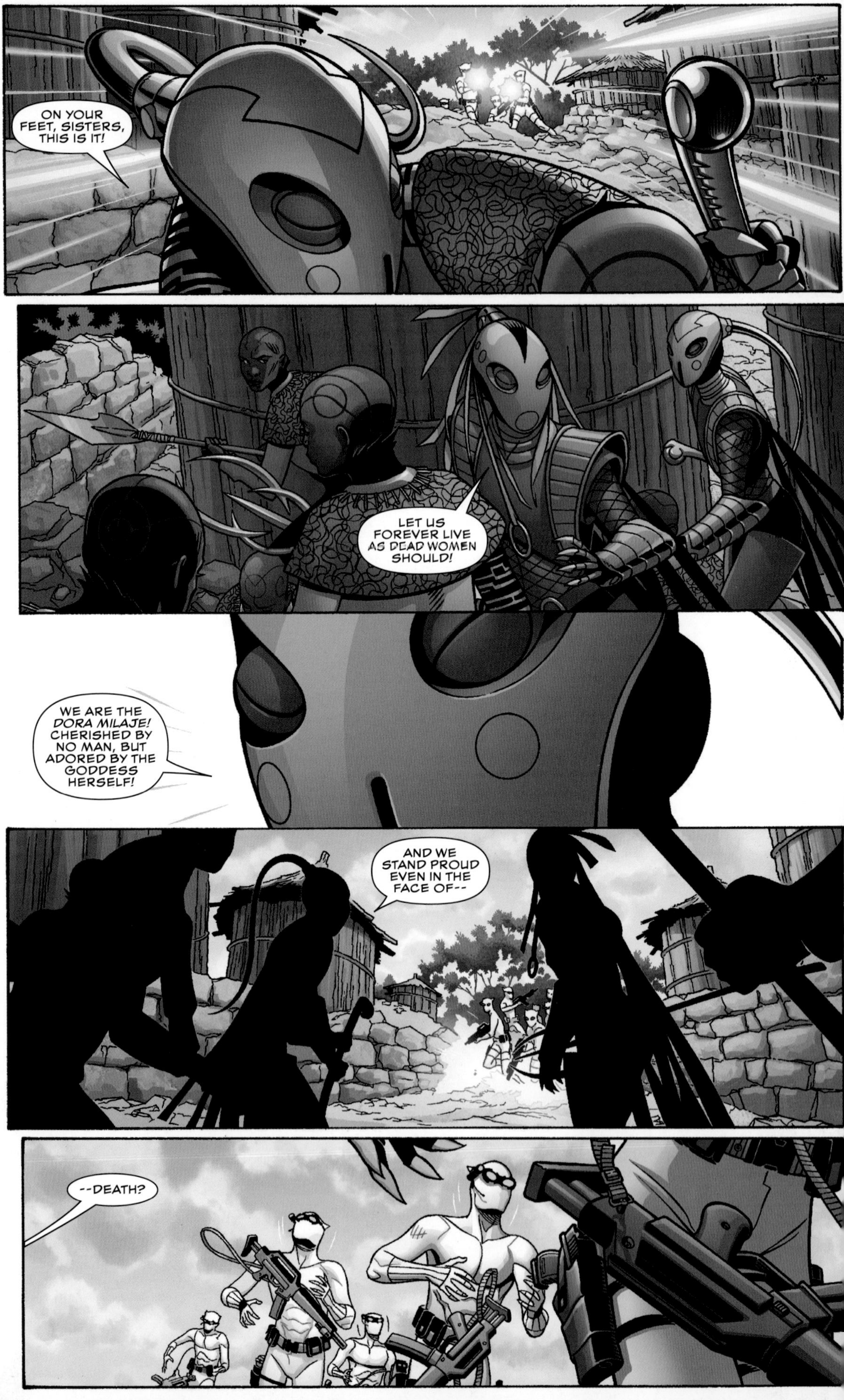
ON YOUR FEET, SISTERS, THIS IS IT!
LET US FOREVER LIVE AS DEAD WOMEN SHOULD!
WE ARE THE *DORA MILAJE!* CHERISHED BY NO MAN, BUT ADORED BY THE GODDESS HERSELF!
AND WE STAND PROUD EVEN IN THE FACE OF--
--DEATH?

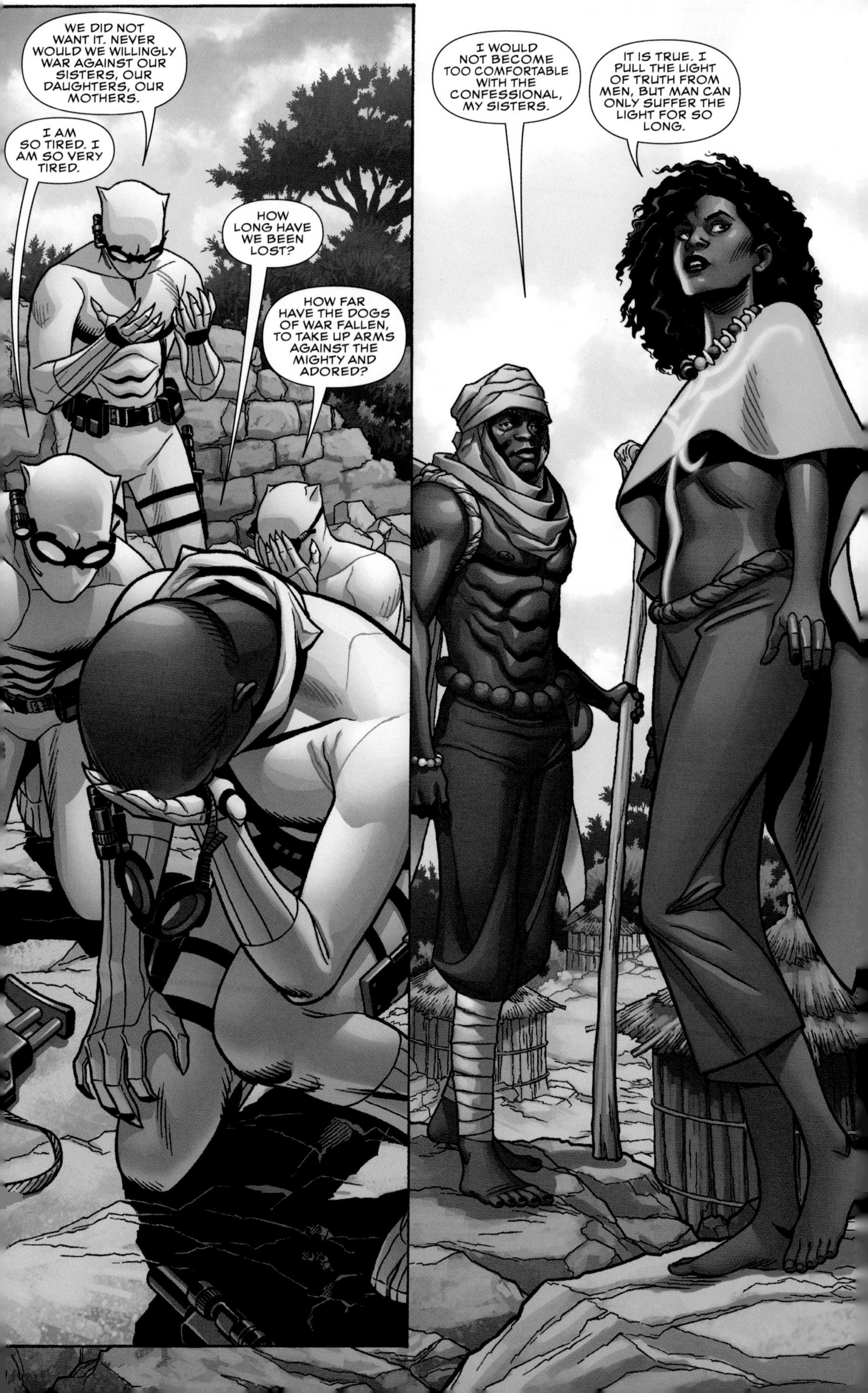
WE DID NOT WANT IT. NEVER WOULD WE WILLINGLY WAR AGAINST OUR SISTERS, OUR DAUGHTERS, OUR MOTHERS.
I AM SO TIRED. I AM SO VERY TIRED.
HOW LONG HAVE WE BEEN LOST?
HOW FAR HAVE THE DOGS OF WAR FALLEN, TO TAKE UP ARMS AGAINST THE MIGHTY AND ADORED?
I WOULD NOT BECOME TOO COMFORTABLE WITH THE CONFESSIONAL, MY SISTERS.
IT IS TRUE. I PULL THE LIGHT OF TRUTH FROM MEN, BUT MAN CAN ONLY SUFFER THE LIGHT FOR SO LONG.

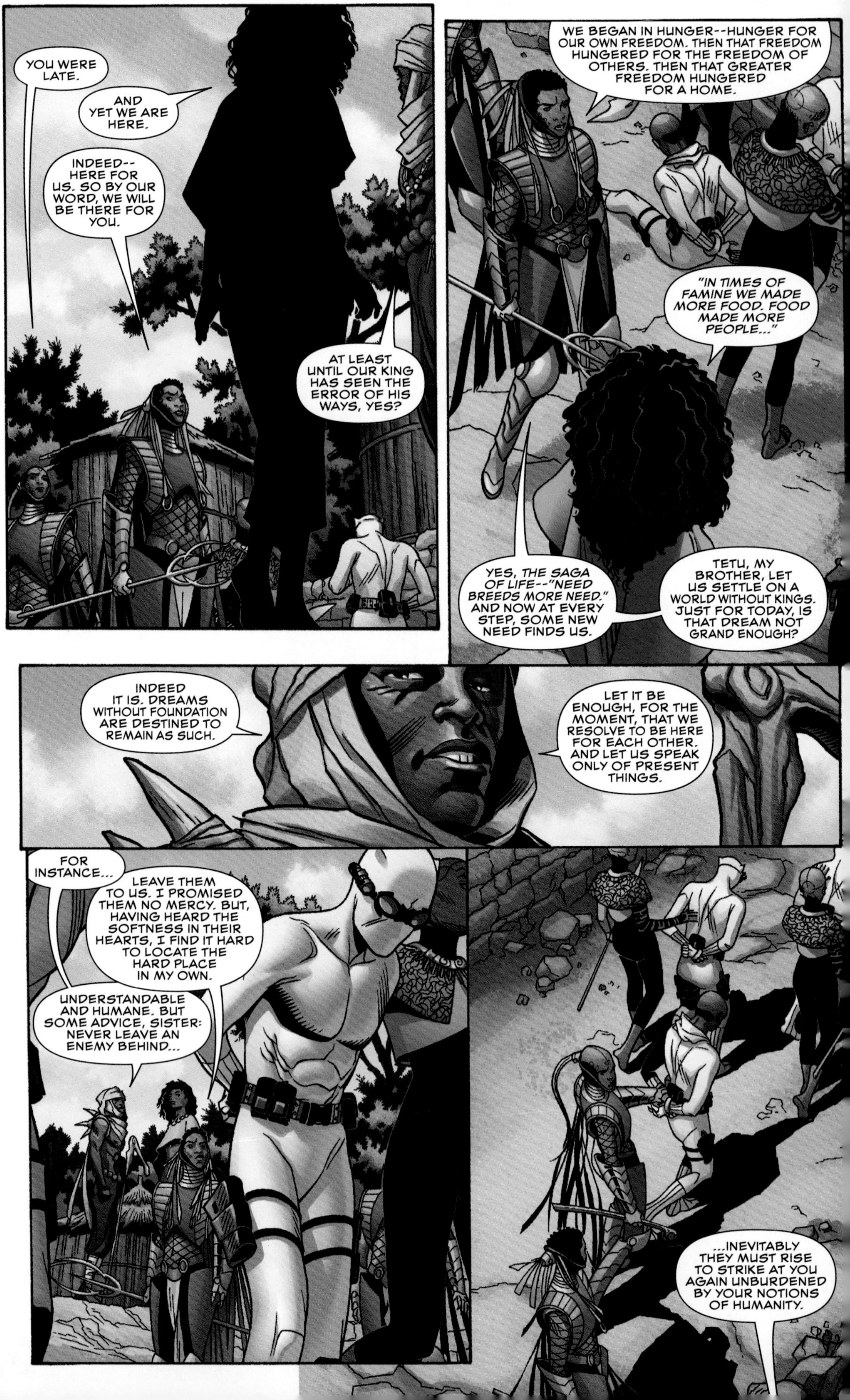
YOU WERE LATE.
AND YET WE ARE HERE.
INDEED-- HERE FOR US. SO BY OUR WORD, WE WILL BE THERE FOR YOU.
AT LEAST UNTIL OUR KING HAS SEEN THE ERROR OF HIS WAYS, YES?
WE BEGAN IN HUNGER--HUNGER FOR OUR OWN FREEDOM. THEN THAT FREEDOM HUNGERED FOR THE FREEDOM OF OTHERS. THEN THAT GREATER FREEDOM HUNGERED FOR A HOME.
"IN TIMES OF FAMINE WE MADE MORE FOOD. FOOD MADE MORE PEOPLE..."
YES, THE SAGA OF LIFE--"NEED BREEDS MORE NEED." AND NOW AT EVERY STEP, SOME NEW NEED FINDS US.
TETU, MY BROTHER, LET US SETTLE ON A WORLD WITHOUT KINGS. JUST FOR TODAY, IS THAT DREAM NOT GRAND ENOUGH?
INDEED IT IS. DREAMS WITHOUT FOUNDATION ARE DESTINED TO REMAIN AS SUCH.
LET IT BE ENOUGH, FOR THE MOMENT, THAT WE RESOLVE TO BE HERE FOR EACH OTHER. AND LET US SPEAK ONLY OF PRESENT THINGS.
FOR INSTANCE...
LEAVE THEM TO US. I PROMISED THEM NO MERCY. BUT, HAVING HEARD THE SOFTNESS IN THEIR HEARTS, I FIND IT HARD TO LOCATE THE HARD PLACE IN MY OWN.
UNDERSTANDABLE AND HUMANE. BUT SOME ADVICE, SISTER: NEVER LEAVE AN ENEMY BEHIND...
...INEVITABLY THEY MUST RISE TO STRIKE AT YOU AGAIN UNBURDENED BY YOUR NOTIONS OF HUMANITY.

NECROPOLIS

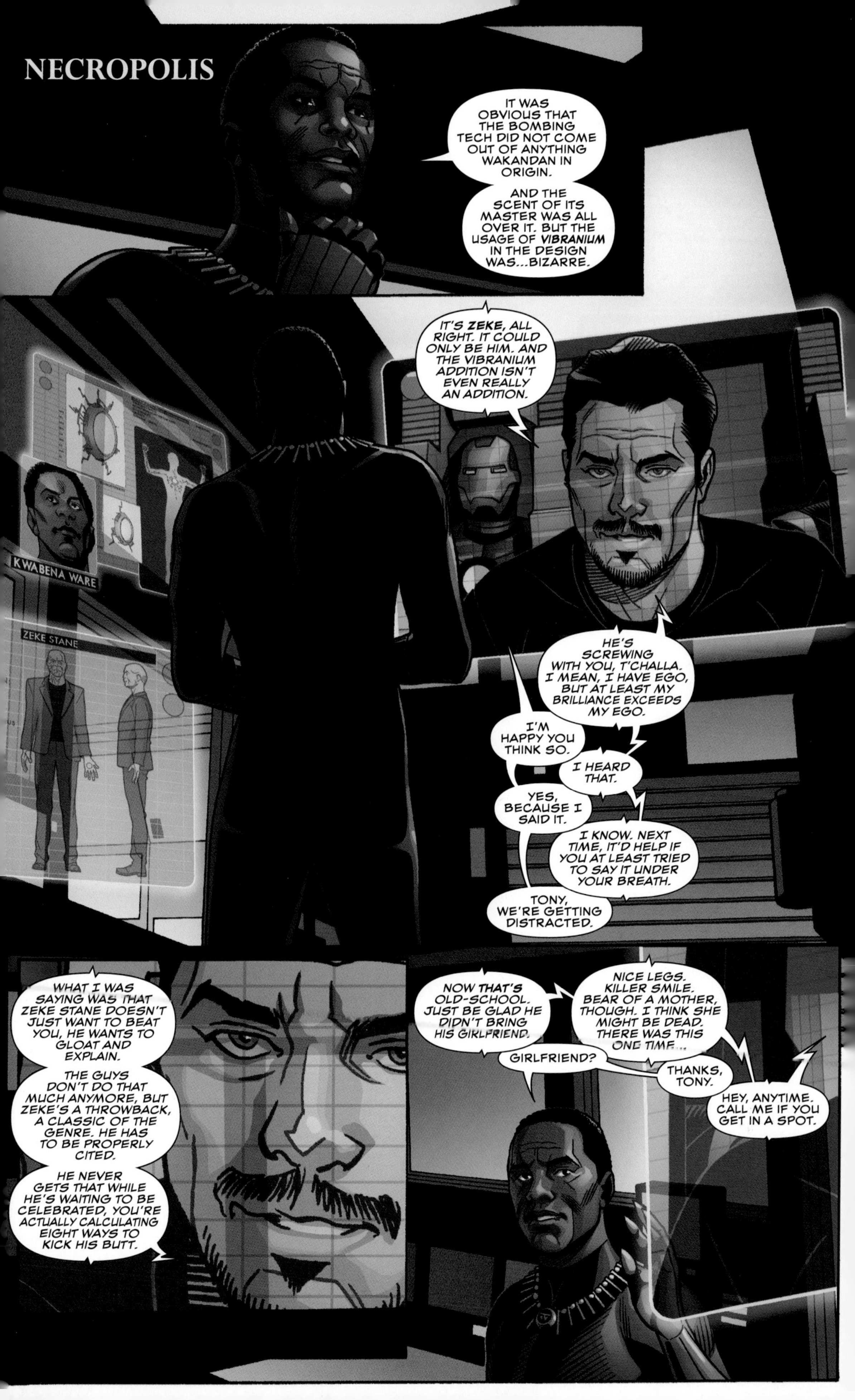
IT WAS OBVIOUS THAT THE BOMBING TECH DID NOT COME OUT OF ANYTHING WAKANDAN IN ORIGIN.
AND THE SCENT OF ITS MASTER WAS ALL OVER IT. BUT THE USAGE OF VIBRANIUM IN THE DESIGN WAS...BIZARRE.
KWABENA WARE
ZEKE STANE
IT'S ZEKE, ALL RIGHT. IT COULD ONLY BE HIM. AND THE VIBRANIUM ADDITION ISN'T EVEN REALLY AN ADDITION.
HE'S SCREWING WITH YOU, T'CHALLA. I MEAN, I HAVE EGO, BUT AT LEAST MY BRILLIANCE EXCEEDS MY EGO.
I'M HAPPY YOU THINK SO.
I HEARD THAT.
YES, BECAUSE I SAID IT.
I KNOW. NEXT TIME, IT'D HELP IF YOU AT LEAST TRIED TO SAY IT UNDER YOUR BREATH.
TONY, WE'RE GETTING DISTRACTED.
WHAT I WAS SAYING WAS THAT ZEKE STANE DOESN'T JUST WANT TO BEAT YOU, HE WANTS TO GLOAT AND EXPLAIN.
THE GUYS DON'T DO THAT MUCH ANYMORE, BUT ZEKE'S A THROWBACK, A CLASSIC OF THE GENRE. HE HAS TO BE PROPERLY CITED.
HE NEVER GETS THAT WHILE HE'S WAITING TO BE CELEBRATED, YOU'RE ACTUALLY CALCULATING EIGHT WAYS TO KICK HIS BUTT.
NOW THAT'S OLD-SCHOOL. JUST BE GLAD HE DIDN'T BRING HIS GIRLFRIEND.
GIRLFRIEND?
NICE LEGS. KILLER SMILE. BEAR OF A MOTHER, THOUGH. I THINK SHE MIGHT BE DEAD. THERE WAS THIS ONE TIME...
THANKS, TONY.
HEY, ANYTIME. CALL ME IF YOU GET IN A SPOT.

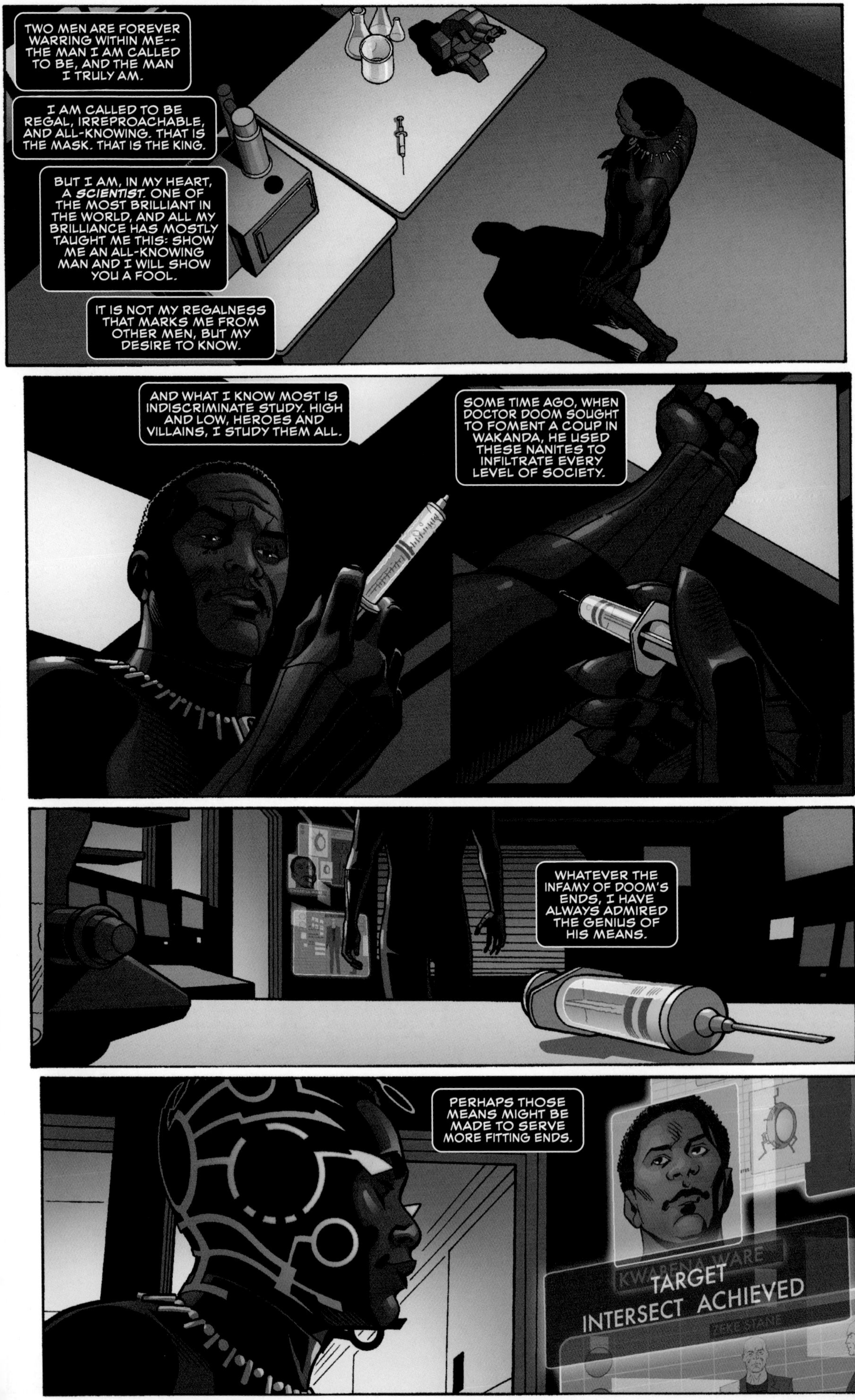
TWO MEN ARE FOREVER WARRING WITHIN ME-- THE MAN I AM CALLED TO BE, AND THE MAN I TRULY AM.
I AM CALLED TO BE REGAL, IRREPROACHABLE, AND ALL-KNOWING. THAT IS THE MASK. THAT IS THE KING.
BUT I AM, IN MY HEART, A *SCIENTIST.* ONE OF THE MOST BRILLIANT IN THE WORLD, AND ALL MY BRILLIANCE HAS MOSTLY TAUGHT ME THIS: SHOW ME AN ALL-KNOWING MAN AND I WILL SHOW YOU A FOOL.
IT IS NOT MY REGALNESS THAT MARKS ME FROM OTHER MEN, BUT MY DESIRE TO KNOW.
AND WHAT I KNOW MOST IS INDISCRIMINATE STUDY. HIGH AND LOW, HEROES AND VILLAINS, I STUDY THEM ALL.
SOME TIME AGO, WHEN DOCTOR DOOM SOUGHT TO FOMENT A COUP IN WAKANDA, HE USED THESE NANITES TO INFILTRATE EVERY LEVEL OF SOCIETY.
WHATEVER THE INFAMY OF DOOM'S ENDS, I HAVE ALWAYS ADMIRED THE GENIUS OF HIS MEANS.
PERHAPS THOSE MEANS MIGHT BE MADE TO SERVE MORE FITTING ENDS.
KWABENA WARE
TARGET INTERSECT ACHIEVED

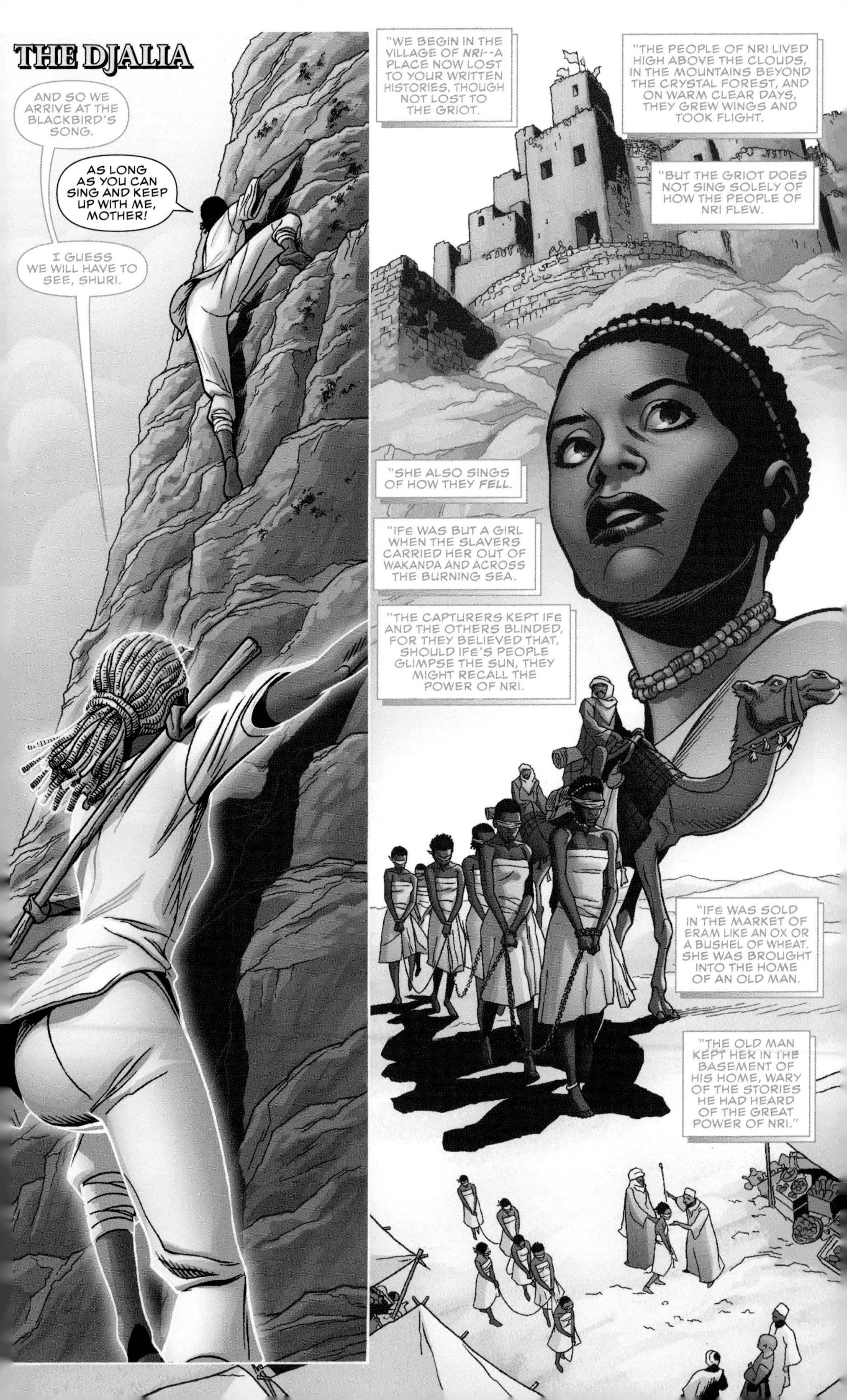
THE DJALIA
AND SO WE ARRIVE AT THE BLACKBIRD'S SONG.
AS LONG AS YOU CAN SING AND KEEP UP WITH ME, MOTHER!
I GUESS WE WILL HAVE TO SEE, SHURI.
"WE BEGIN IN THE VILLAGE OF NRI--A PLACE NOW LOST TO YOUR WRITTEN HISTORIES, THOUGH NOT LOST TO THE GRIOT.
"THE PEOPLE OF NRI LIVED HIGH ABOVE THE CLOUDS, IN THE MOUNTAINS BEYOND THE CRYSTAL FOREST, AND ON WARM CLEAR DAYS, THEY GREW WINGS AND TOOK FLIGHT.
"BUT THE GRIOT DOES NOT SING SOLELY OF HOW THE PEOPLE OF NRI FLEW.
"SHE ALSO SINGS OF HOW THEY FELL.
"IFE WAS BUT A GIRL WHEN THE SLAVERS CARRIED HER OUT OF WAKANDA AND ACROSS THE BURNING SEA.
"THE CAPTURERS KEPT IFE AND THE OTHERS BLINDED, FOR THEY BELIEVED THAT, SHOULD IFE'S PEOPLE GLIMPSE THE SUN, THEY MIGHT RECALL THE POWER OF NRI.
"IFE WAS SOLD IN THE MARKET OF ERAM LIKE AN OX OR A BUSHEL OF WHEAT. SHE WAS BROUGHT INTO THE HOME OF AN OLD MAN.
"THE OLD MAN KEPT HER IN THE BASEMENT OF HIS HOME, WARY OF THE STORIES HE HAD HEARD OF THE GREAT POWER OF NRI."

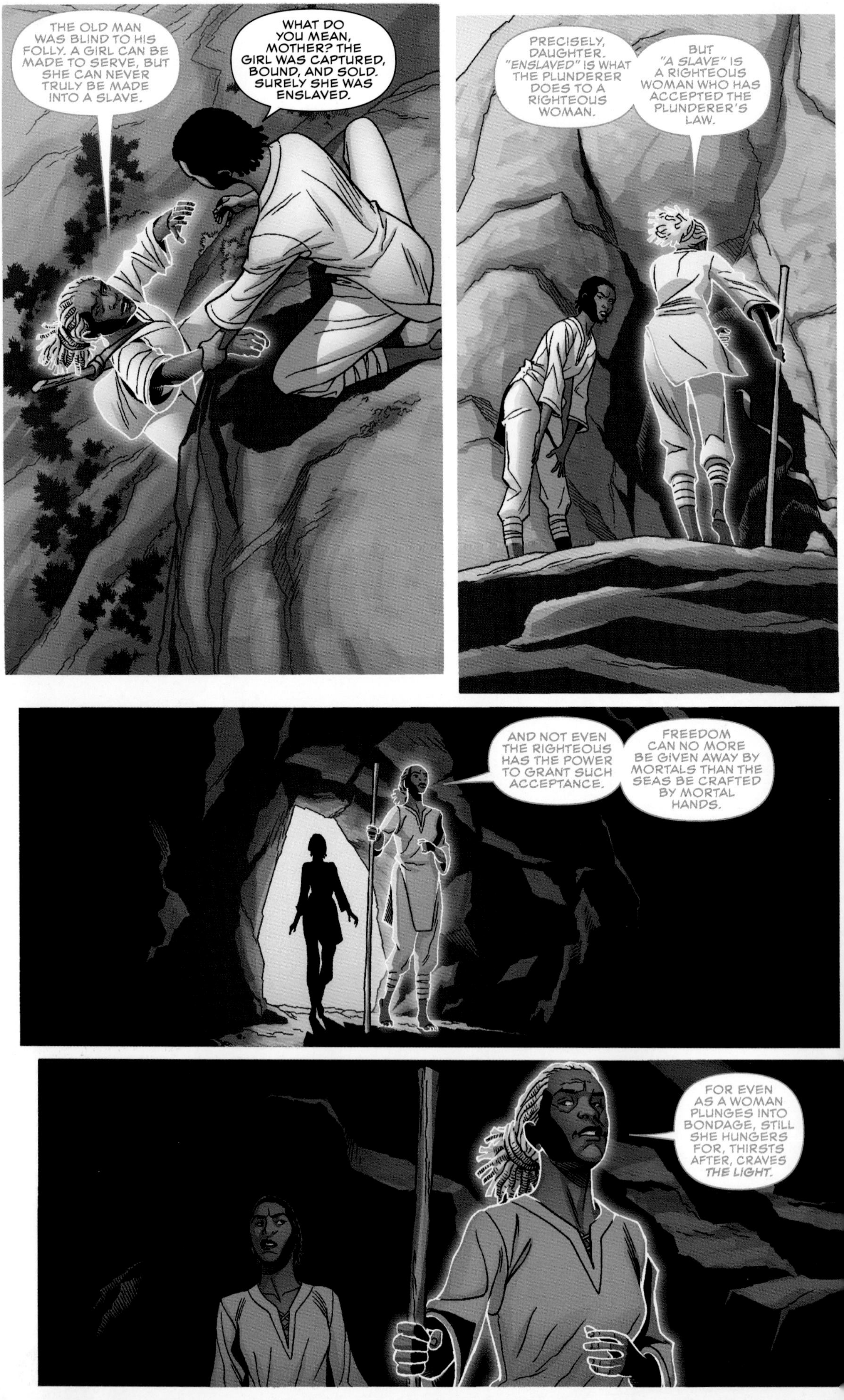
THE OLD MAN WAS BLIND TO HIS FOLLY. A GIRL CAN BE MADE TO SERVE, BUT SHE CAN NEVER TRULY BE MADE INTO A SLAVE.
WHAT DO YOU MEAN, MOTHER? THE GIRL WAS CAPTURED, BOUND, AND SOLD. SURELY SHE WAS ENSLAVED.
PRECISELY, DAUGHTER. "ENSLAVED" IS WHAT THE PLUNDERER DOES TO A RIGHTEOUS WOMAN.
BUT "A SLAVE" IS A RIGHTEOUS WOMAN WHO HAS ACCEPTED THE PLUNDERER'S LAW.
AND NOT EVEN THE RIGHTEOUS HAS THE POWER TO GRANT SUCH ACCEPTANCE.
FREEDOM CAN NO MORE BE GIVEN AWAY BY MORTALS THAN THE SEAS BE CRAFTED BY MORTAL HANDS.
FOR EVEN AS A WOMAN PLUNGES INTO BONDAGE, STILL SHE HUNGERS FOR, THIRSTS AFTER, CRAVES THE LIGHT.

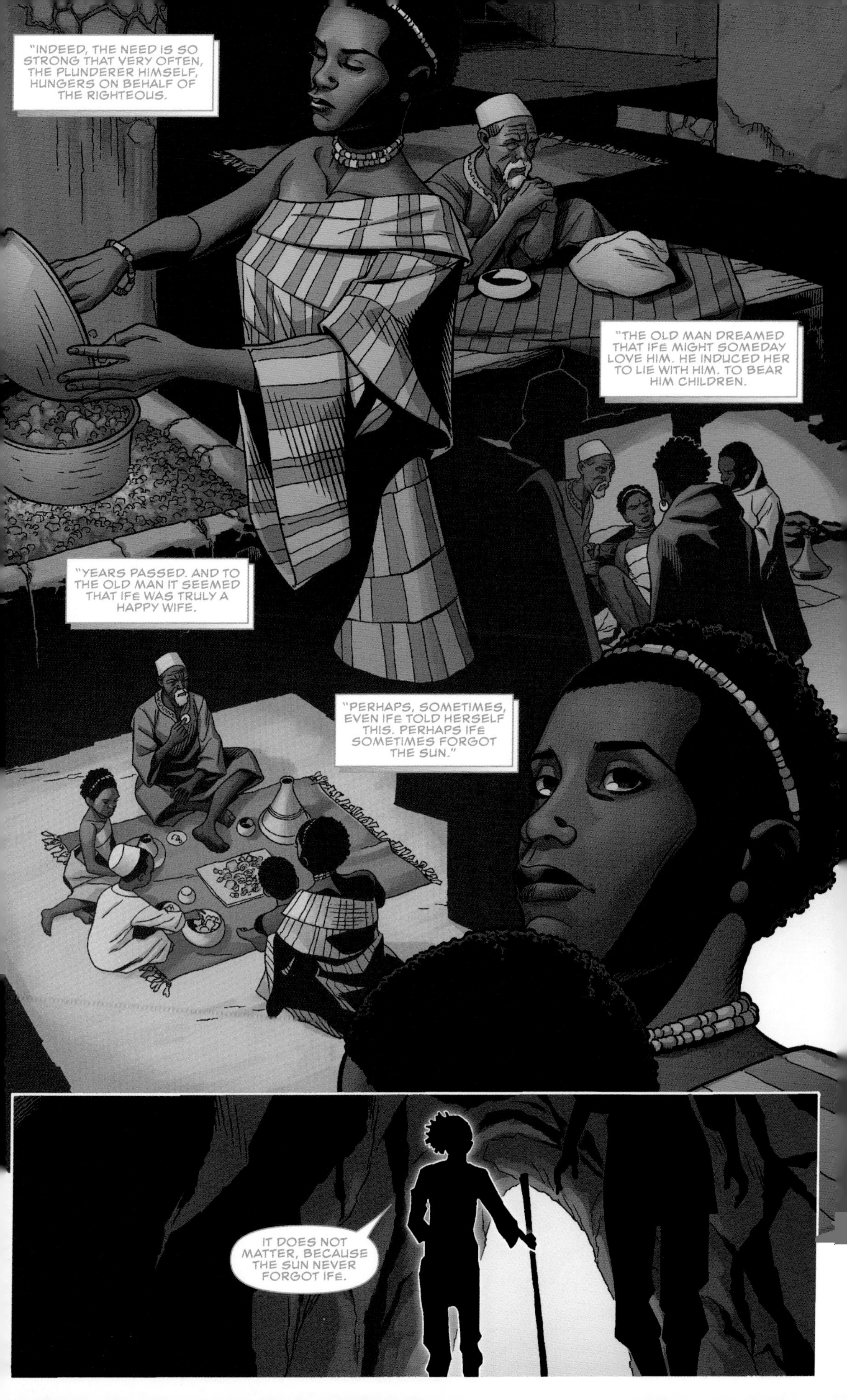
"INDEED, THE NEED IS SO STRONG THAT VERY OFTEN, THE PLUNDERER HIMSELF, HUNGERS ON BEHALF OF THE RIGHTEOUS.
"THE OLD MAN DREAMED THAT IFE MIGHT SOMEDAY LOVE HIM. HE INDUCED HER TO LIE WITH HIM. TO BEAR HIM CHILDREN.
"YEARS PASSED. AND TO THE OLD MAN IT SEEMED THAT IFE WAS TRULY A HAPPY WIFE.
"PERHAPS, SOMETIMES, EVEN IFE TOLD HERSELF THIS. PERHAPS IFE SOMETIMES FORGOT THE SUN."
IT DOES NOT MATTER, BECAUSE THE SUN NEVER FORGOT IFE.

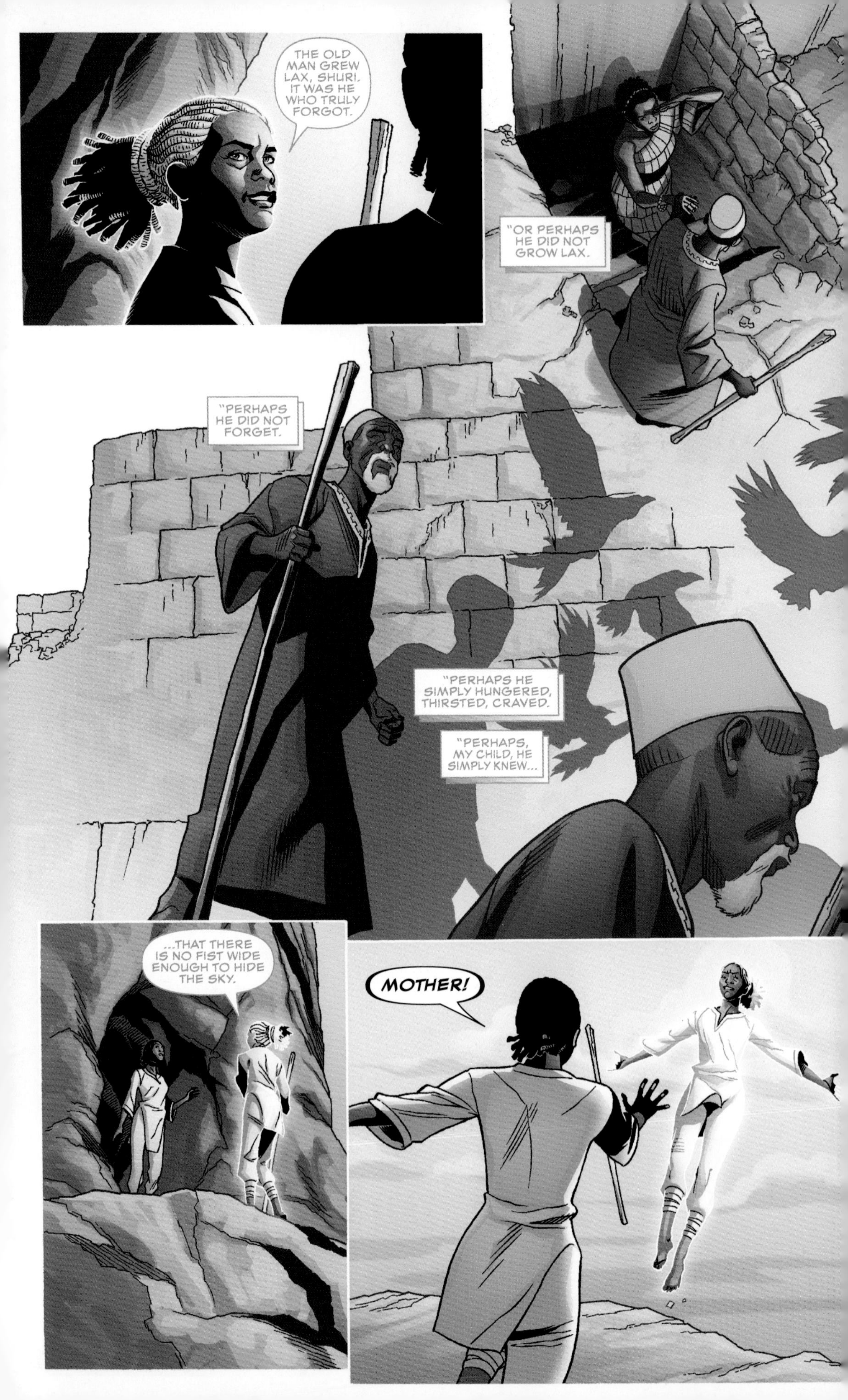
THE OLD MAN GREW LAX, SHURI. IT WAS HE WHO TRULY FORGOT.
"OR PERHAPS HE DID NOT GROW LAX.
"PERHAPS HE DID NOT FORGET.
"PERHAPS HE SIMPLY HUNGERED, THIRSTED, CRAVED.
"PERHAPS, MY CHILD, HE SIMPLY KNEW...
...THAT THERE IS NO FIST WIDE ENOUGH TO HIDE THE SKY.
MOTHER!

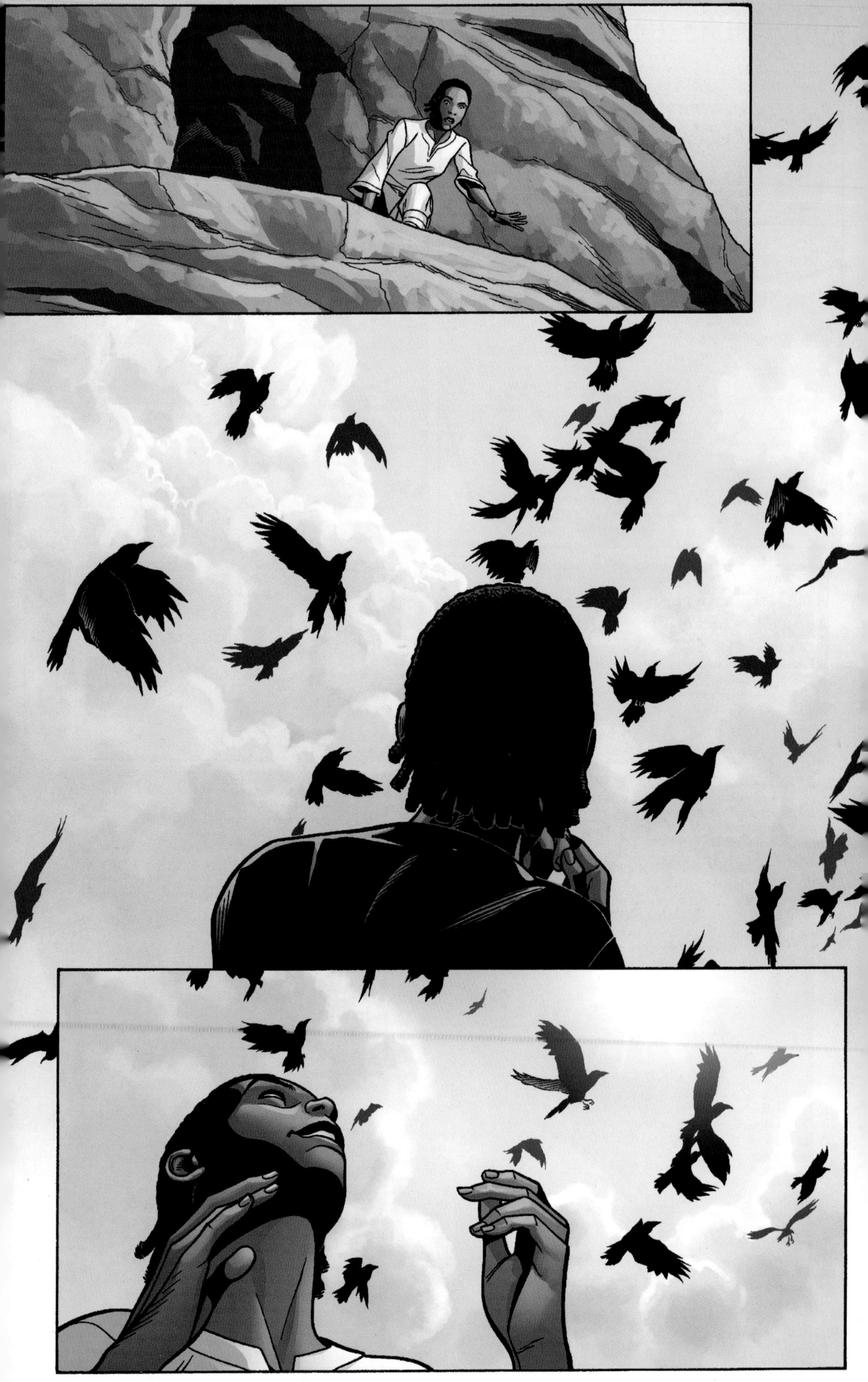

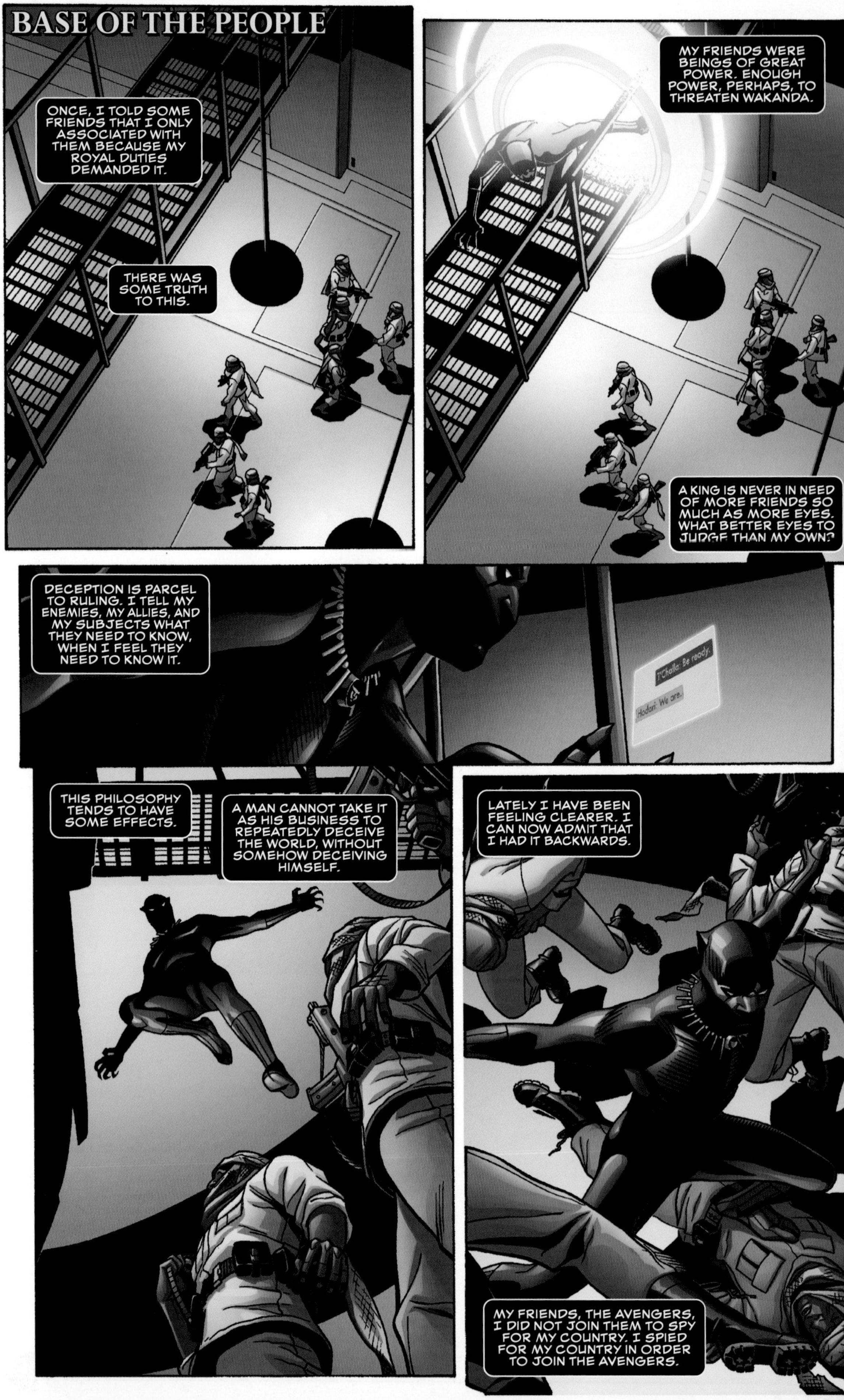
BASE OF THE PEOPLE
ONCE, I TOLD SOME FRIENDS THAT I ONLY ASSOCIATED WITH THEM BECAUSE MY ROYAL DUTIES DEMANDED IT.
THERE WAS SOME TRUTH TO THIS.
MY FRIENDS WERE BEINGS OF GREAT POWER. ENOUGH POWER, PERHAPS, TO THREATEN WAKANDA.
A KING IS NEVER IN NEED OF MORE FRIENDS SO MUCH AS MORE EYES. WHAT BETTER EYES TO JUDGE THAN MY OWN?
DECEPTION IS PARCEL TO RULING. I TELL MY ENEMIES, MY ALLIES, AND MY SUBJECTS WHAT THEY NEED TO KNOW, WHEN I FEEL THEY NEED TO KNOW IT.
T'Challa: Be ready.
Hodari: We are.
THIS PHILOSOPHY TENDS TO HAVE SOME EFFECTS.
A MAN CANNOT TAKE IT AS HIS BUSINESS TO REPEATEDLY DECEIVE THE WORLD, WITHOUT SOMEHOW DECEIVING HIMSELF.
LATELY I HAVE BEEN FEELING CLEARER. I CAN NOW ADMIT THAT I HAD IT BACKWARDS.
MY FRIENDS, THE AVENGERS, I DID NOT JOIN THEM TO SPY FOR MY COUNTRY. I SPIED FOR MY COUNTRY IN ORDER TO JOIN THE AVENGERS.

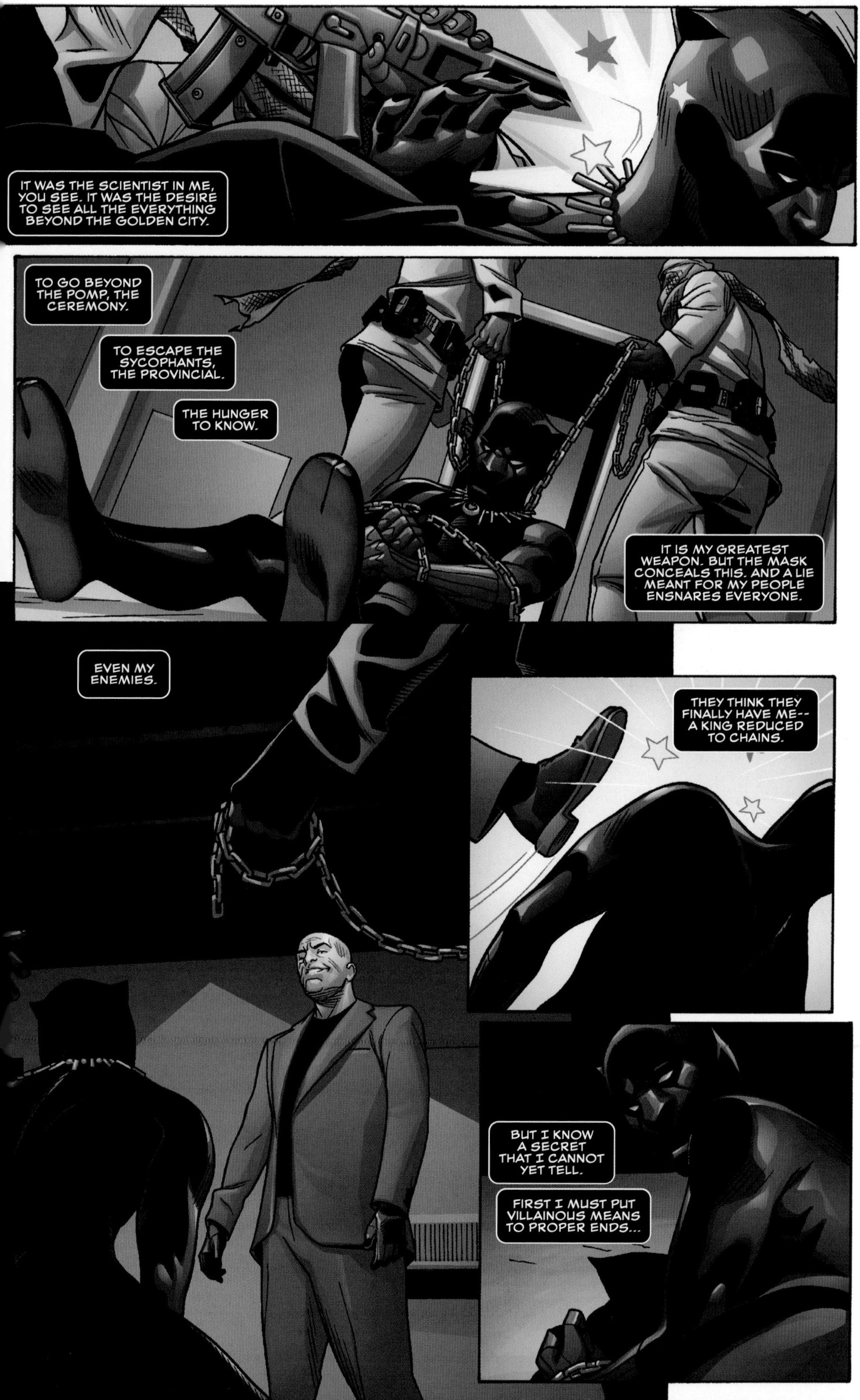
IT WAS THE SCIENTIST IN ME, YOU SEE. IT WAS THE DESIRE TO SEE ALL THE EVERYTHING BEYOND THE GOLDEN CITY.
TO GO BEYOND THE POMP, THE CEREMONY.
TO ESCAPE THE SYCOPHANTS, THE PROVINCIAL.
THE HUNGER TO KNOW.
IT IS MY GREATEST WEAPON. BUT THE MASK CONCEALS THIS. AND A LIE MEANT FOR MY PEOPLE ENSNARES EVERYONE.
EVEN MY ENEMIES.
THEY THINK THEY FINALLY HAVE ME-- A KING REDUCED TO CHAINS.
BUT I KNOW A SECRET THAT I CANNOT YET TELL.
FIRST I MUST PUT VILLAINOUS MEANS TO PROPER ENDS...

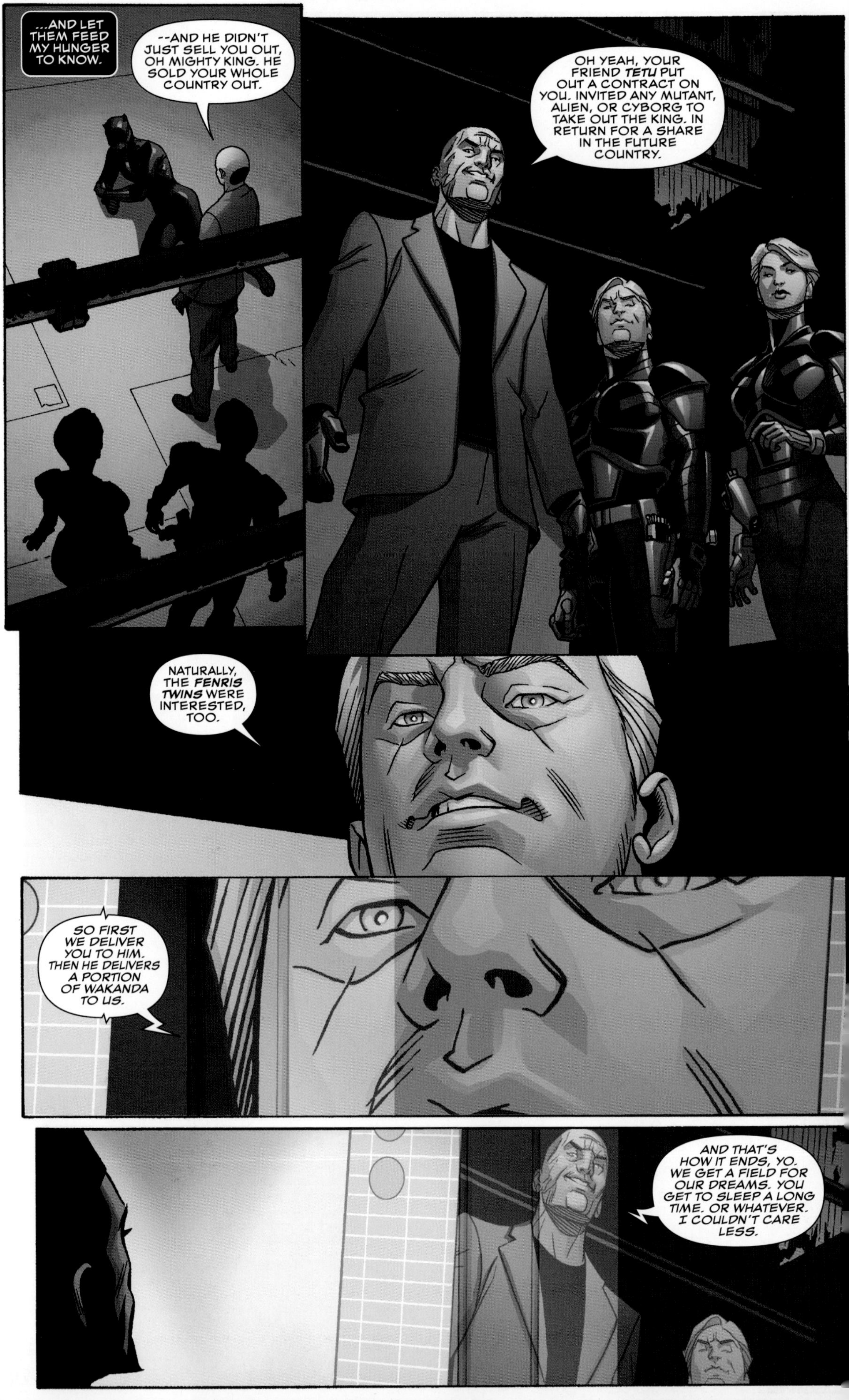
...AND LET THEM FEED MY HUNGER TO KNOW.
--AND HE DIDN'T JUST SELL YOU OUT, OH MIGHTY KING. HE SOLD YOUR WHOLE COUNTRY OUT.
OH YEAH, YOUR FRIEND TETU PUT OUT A CONTRACT ON YOU. INVITED ANY MUTANT, ALIEN, OR CYBORG TO TAKE OUT THE KING. IN RETURN FOR A SHARE IN THE FUTURE COUNTRY.
NATURALLY, THE FENRIS TWINS WERE INTERESTED, TOO.
SO FIRST WE DELIVER YOU TO HIM. THEN HE DELIVERS A PORTION OF WAKANDA TO US.
AND THAT'S HOW IT ENDS, YO. WE GET A FIELD FOR OUR DREAMS. YOU GET TO SLEEP A LONG TIME. OR WHATEVER. I COULDN'T CARE LESS.

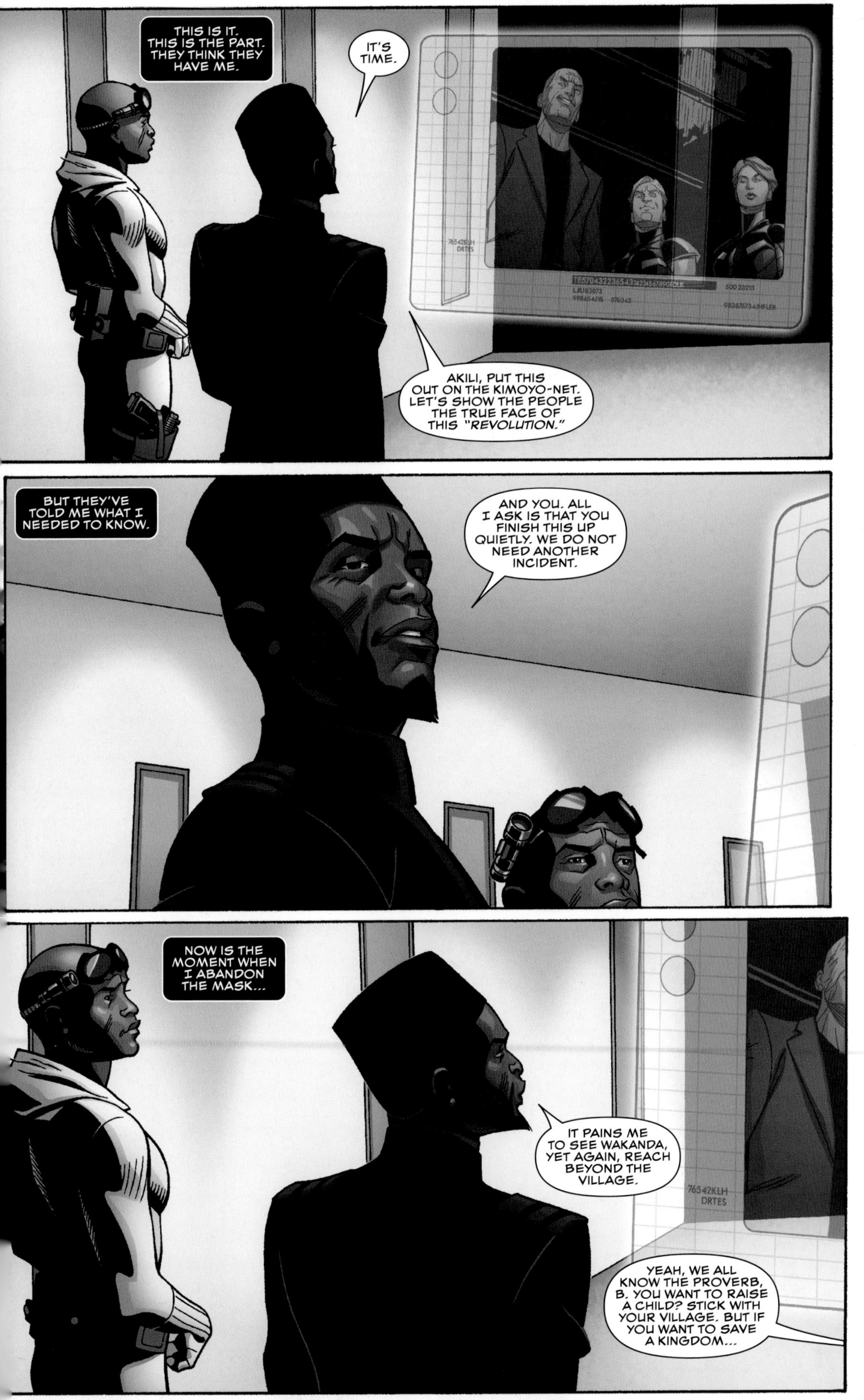
THIS IS IT. THIS IS THE PART. THEY THINK THEY HAVE ME.
IT'S TIME.
AKILI, PUT THIS OUT ON THE KIMOYO-NET. LET'S SHOW THE PEOPLE THE TRUE FACE OF THIS "*REVOLUTION.*"
BUT THEY'VE TOLD ME WHAT I NEEDED TO KNOW.
AND YOU. ALL I ASK IS THAT YOU FINISH THIS UP QUIETLY. WE DO NOT NEED ANOTHER INCIDENT.
NOW IS THE MOMENT WHEN I ABANDON THE MASK...
IT PAINS ME TO SEE WAKANDA, YET AGAIN, REACH BEYOND THE VILLAGE.
76542KLH DRTES
YEAH, WE ALL KNOW THE PROVERB, B. YOU WANT TO RAISE A CHILD? STICK WITH YOUR VILLAGE. BUT IF YOU WANT TO SAVE A KINGDOM...

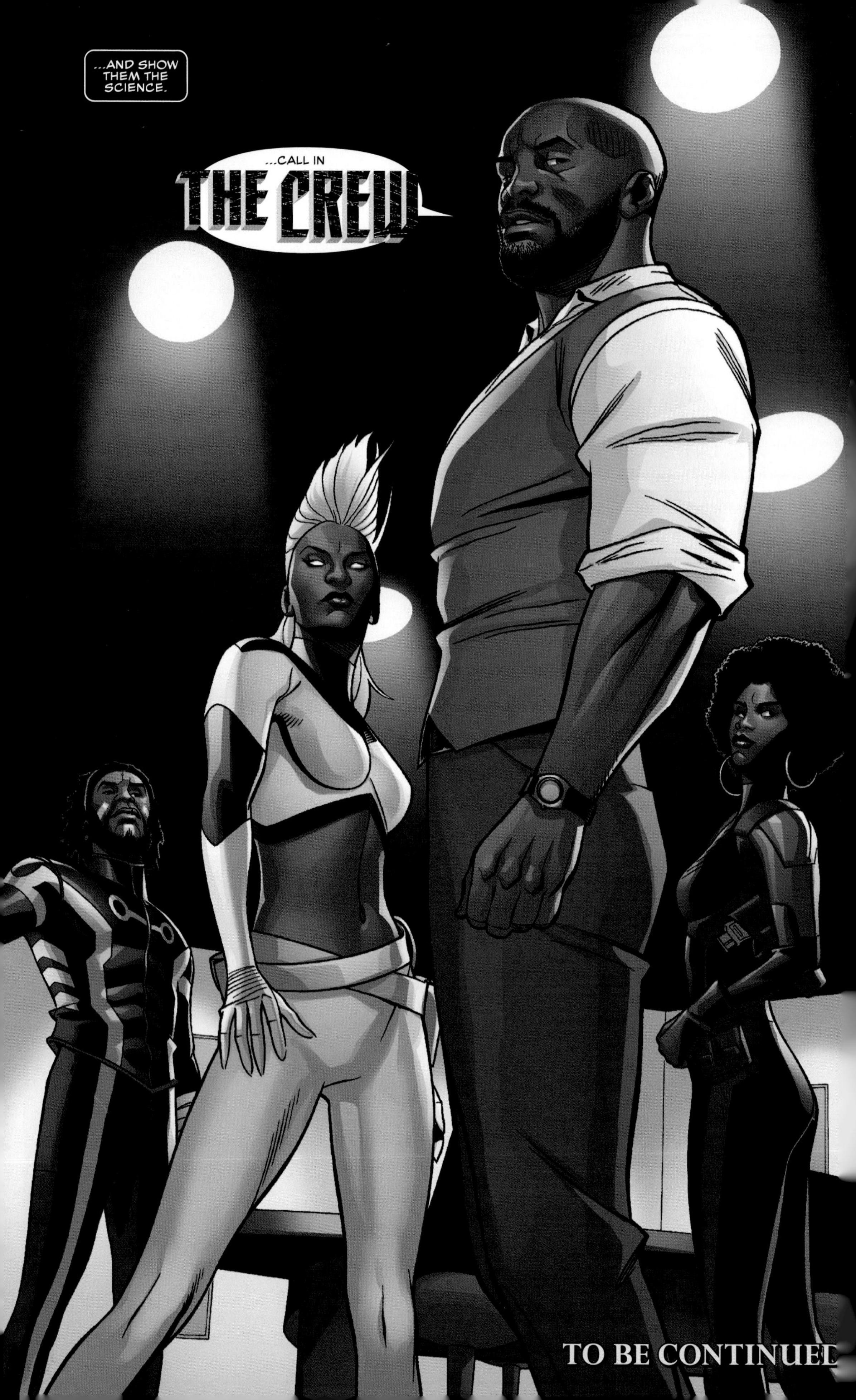
...AND SHOW THEM THE SCIENCE.
...CALL IN THE CREW
TO BE CONTINUED